PENGUIN BOOKS
A NECKLACE OF SKULLS

Eunice de Souza (1940–2017) was born in Pune where she grew up. She graduated from the University of Bombay, did her postgraduate work at Marquette University in the US and later obtained a doctorate for her thesis on Indian poetry and criticism from the University of Bombay. She taught English literature at St. Xavier's College, Mumbai, and was head of the department till she retired. There she organized poetry readings and was later involved in setting up of the well-known literary festival 'Ithaka'.

She was the author of several books of poems. Her groundbreaking book of poems *Fix* was published in 1979, followed by *Women in Dutch Painting* (1988), *Ways of Belonging* (1990) and *Learn from the Almond Leaf* (2016). She also wrote two novels—*Dangerlok* (2001) and *Dev and Simran* (2003)—several books for children, and edited several poetry anthologies, the last of which, *These My Words: The Penguin Book of Indian Poetry* (2012), she co-edited with Melanie Silgardo. In the last several years of her life she brought all the weight of her knowledge to her much-loved weekly *Mumbai Mirror* column on reading and literature which she wrote right to the end.

PRAISE FOR THE BOOK

'Eunice de Souza's poems have an accuracy of detail and something of the quality of photographs taken at a decisive moment—with individuals or groups fixed at their most acute moments of pretension, cruelty or loneliness—that make them memorable. The more introspective poems [are] no less sharply focused. In them the poet bears pain, however personal, not by the usual literary expediency of diffusing it but by mercilessly bringing it to light'—Adil Jussawalla

'*A Necklace of Skulls* is nothing less than the collected work of a pioneer . . . It will survive in the language of the mind, the vernacular in the deep sense, because that is the language in which she has, with unerring instinct, chosen to write it'—Anjum Hasan, *Caravan*

'If Kamala Das brought female sexuality into Indian verse, de Souza ushered in female rage—a white-hot, page-searing, bone-chilling fury'— Arundhathi Subramaniam, *The Hindu*

'What struck me at once about the poems was their immediacy, their complete impact, their unguarded sense of statement . . . There is a marvellous irony, delicately and at the same time savagely handled . . . I have been moved by these poems which have such directness, vigour and such a strange mixture of triumph, vision and agony'—A.D. Hope

EUNICE DE SOUZA

A Necklace of Skulls

collected poems

Foreword by Melanie Silgardo

PENGUIN BOOKS

An imprint of Penguin Random House

PENGUIN BOOKS

USA | Canada | UK | Ireland | Australia
New Zealand | India | South Africa | China

Penguin Books is part of the Penguin Random House group of companies
whose addresses can be found at global.penguinrandomhouse.com

Published by Penguin Random House India Pvt. Ltd
4th Floor, Capital Tower 1, MG Road,
Gurugram 122 002, Haryana, India

Penguin
Random House
India

First published by Penguin Books India 2009
This edition published 2019

Copyright © Melanie Silgardo 2019

Fix was first published by Newground, Mumbai, 1979
Women in Dutch Painting was first published by Praxis, Mumbai, 1988
Ways of Belonging: Selected Poems was first published by Polygon, Edinburgh, 1990
Selected and New Poems was first published by St. Xavier's College, Mumbai, 1994
Dangerlok was first published by Penguin Books India, New Delhi, 2001

All rights reserved

10 9 8 7 6 5 4 3 2

ISBN 9780143068150

Typeset in Weiss by Eleven Arts, New Delhi
Printed at Repro India Limited

www.penguin.co.in

For Melanie Silgardo, and for Adil and Veronik Jussawalla

Contents

Contents

Contents

From *Ways of Belonging: Selected Poems* (1990)

Contents

Foreword

When Eunice de Souza died in July 2017 she left little that required tidying up or sorting out. She had organized her papers—letters, reviews, certificates, ephemera—neatly into folders, photos into albums; had given away to friends things precious to her: pictures, paintings, furniture. Her last volume of poetry had been published the year before with urgency. Fiercely independent to the last, despite her failing health, she had got herself into a state of preparedness. *Learn from the Almond Leaf*, a slim, elegiac volume full of agonizing presentiment ('Tell me, Mr Death/ Date. Time. Place.'; 'Earth is tired./ Her bones creak and grind') was a tying up of loose ends, a saying goodbye. This collection, *A Necklace of Skulls*, predating it by several years, is a collection of her complete earlier poems, including her pioneering first book of poems, *Fix*.

To write this Foreword to *A Necklace of Skulls* which Penguin are reissuing is a great personal privilege. For me, Eunice's death marked not just the end of a life-long friendship, but the end of an institution that was Eunice de Souza. I had known her for more than forty years, first as a student, then publisher and friend. When we published *Fix* in 1979 we knew we were putting into print a volume of poetry that was quite different from anything around. Eunice, though, felt unsure of the poems, wondered whether they were poems at all. Validation came from some of her closest contemporaries and friends. For Adil Jussawalla, writing on the cover of *Fix*, the poems had 'an accuracy of detail and something of the quality of photographs taken at a decisive moment'; for Arvind Krishna Mehrotra, writing in the introduction to her poems in *Twelve Indian Poets*, they had 'the brevity, unexpectedness and urgency of telegrams'.

Fix was first published in 1979 by Newground. Clearing House had scheduled it for their next batch but Eunice was impatient; the manuscript had been lying around too long and she wanted it out there. Santan Rodrigues, Raul da Gama Rose and I had just published *Three Poets*, ourselves, in Newground's first ever volume. It was based on the Clearing House model and was a success. When I suggested to Eunice that we might publish her her response was immediate and unequivocal. Arun Kolatkar's cover design for *Fix* was magnificent—stark and bold—an almost life-size portrait of Eunice in silvered black and white, cropped close around the head, her gaze direct, unflinching, her forehead marked with a cross or an X, calling to mind the iconography of mug shots, of prisoners about to do time. It was a groundbreaking volume of poems— original, punchy, daring, seething with rage, undercut with self-irony. From the very first poem, 'Catholic Mother', she was to establish her poetic DNA as she excoriated hypocrisy and pretension, whether in the community, family or relationships.

> We've had seven children
> (in seven years)
> [...]
> Pillar of the Church
> says the parish priest

> Lovely Catholic Family
> says Mother Superior
>
> the pillar's wife
> says nothing.

These were poems that didn't just pick and prod at the Goan Catholic community, but were nuanced with the registers of sympathy ('Miss Louise') and irony ('Conversation Piece'), and had rippling underneath a dark and visceral vision and a deeply emotional literacy ('Forgive Me, Mother'). Self-awareness, guilt, forgiveness and reparation were to be recurring themes:

> Poems can have order, sanity,
> aesthetic distance from the debris,
> All I've learnt from pain
> I always knew,
> but could not do. ('Don't Look for My Life in These Poems')

She never baulked at using her life, her curiosity, her engagement with lovers, friends, students, retainers as her material. But her poems transcended the personal, the 'confessional'—she gave them context and moral perspective with a lightness, dryness, irreverence and humour that became her hallmark. She always maintained she never set out to write like this, she just did: 'Just keep at what you are:/ a sour old puss in verse/ and leave the rest to me.'

A Necklace of Skulls charts her transition from *Fix*, through to her later volumes—*Women in Dutch Painting* and *Ways of*

Belonging—and poems unpublished in any of these volumes. For a writing life spanning more than forty years her output was lean, pared-down. Every word and every line was turned over, inspected for the superfluous ('Even this poem/has forty-eight words too many' ['It's Time to Find a Place']). That was how she wrote. Even when she was working on her weekly column for the *Mumbai Mirror* in the days before, she would sit in front of her laptop and would be what she always called 'mulling', waiting for the ideas, the intersections, the connections, the clarity. In her final volume *Learn from the Almond Leaf* (Poetrywala 2016), she delighted in saying the poems came in the wee hours of the morning when her restless dog would drag her out of bed for a walk in the compound, when the not-yet dawn and unusual quiet of her bustling neighbourhood forged whole poems in her head that she hastily dashed down in an exercise book.

She honed and whittled till she got to the nub of things. Her language was always precise, her cadence colloquial, her punctuation minimal, her ear exact. She used the voice and persona to great effect and she was master of the nuanced line. She often quoted Robert Browning's poem *My Last Duchess* as having a lasting influence on her. She admired the scope of the dramatic monologue, the changes in tone and voice, the suggestion and the loaded yet unsaid statement—all elements she would come to use herself. Unlike Browning, she used form and structure casually but with just as deadly effect.

The death of her father when she was three haunted her throughout her life. It was a loss she never really recovered from and many of her poems are charged with symbols and recurring images referencing this loss—monsoons, mists, blue hills—a chilling pull towards oblivion and then the coming up for air—as in:

> It's too late for me
> to die young
> as you did
> [...] I cling to little things—
> a glossy new leaf
> a singing bird at dawn
> [...] I convince myself
> [...] that living does not desecrate
> your memory. ('Untitled')

or

> You are the cold wind
> The grey mist.
> The black dawn.
> The grinning skull.
> I am you. ('For My Father, Dead Young')

She writes about childhood with a piercing nostalgia: 'In school/ I clutched Sister Flora's skirt/ and cried for my mother/ who taught across the road/ Sister Flora is dead/ The school is still standing/ I am still learning/ to cross the road' ('The Road (for Deepak Ananth)'). The issues of belonging, difference and abandonment permeate her poems. From the wider cultural context to the more personal ('I've heard it said/ my parents wanted a boy' ['de Souza Prabhu']) her vein of feminism runs all the way through—even scolding Tukaram

('You made life hard for your wife/ and I'm not sure I approve of that' ['Return']).

In *Women in Dutch Painting* and *Ways of Belonging* she moves into a more introspective space, but no less challenging. She circles the self, offers advice peppered with the right amount of wit and spite ('Keep cats/ if you want to learn to cope with/ the otherness of lovers'), writes love poems that bite ('I choose not to marry you, love./ There is poison in my tongue'). Then there are poems such as 'Songs of Innocence', one of my favourites, where she casts her net wide from banal kindergarten Bible study to the deeply moving foraging for ancestral roots to establish a sense of belonging. In the poem 'Notations' in *Ways of Belonging* she harks back to an oral tradition where less is more and where loss permeates everything: 'It happened: that is all they say. It happened.' She saw the Bhakti poets, Tukaram in particular, and the women poets in general as her literary ancestors. Like them she could write about the minutiae of daily life and the vastness of the universe in the space of a few lines ('So you are going too, my love,/ the last, most beautiful/ of my children/ [...] One sets them free——/ to learn, finally learn/ to claim nothing'). She was a poet whose touchstone was the honest, the authentic, the unguarded self. She left us a small but potent legacy—poems that will survive us all.

Melanie Silgardo, 2019

Preface

I'd like to thank Ravi Singh for suggesting this volume of collected poems. My books, like those of many other poets, have not been available for years and readers have had to depend on anthologies. In any case, *Ways of Belonging*, which was published by Polygon in Edinburgh, has never been available in India.

I'd also like to thank the poets' cooperatives which published my first book *Fix* in 1979 (Arun Kolatkar designed the cover), and the second, *Women in Dutch Painting*, in 1988. Santan Rodrigues, Melanie Silgardo and Raul da Gama Rose formed Newground which published their own book, *Three Poets*, and several others including *Fix*. Adil Jussawalla was in charge of Praxis which published *Women in Dutch Painting*. *Ways of Belonging* and *Selected and New Poems* (Department of English, St. Xavier's College, Mumbai) included many of the poems from the first two books, but also contained new sections. My novella *Dangerlok*, published by Penguin Books India in 2001, also contains some poems. In the present volume I've included some early poems, which for reasons I cannot remember were not published, and some new ones too. The poem 'Alibi' which should have been in *Fix* was left out at the time, mainly because I had this vision of reviewers using one of the phrases from the poem as their title, 'a sour old puss in verse'.

I haven't kept track of exactly when I wrote each poem, but there is one date I do remember—28 August 1971, Adil and Veronik Jussawalla's wedding day. I couldn't be part of their celebrations as I was ill, and it was pouring anyway. But I sent them one of the poems I had just written, a thoroughly unsuitable one—'Marriages Are Made'. I first met Adil in London in the sixties, the same time when I first met Farrukh Dhondy, though he lived down the street from me in Poona, and when I caught up again with Mala Sen, Darryl D'Monte and their circle of friends. Adil and Veronik were endlessly supportive when I lived in a grungy paying-guest room in Colaba.

Earlier, on my return from the US where I did my graduate work, I met Nissim Ezekiel when he interviewed me for a teaching job. He assured me I would be unhappy at the college he represented so I didn't take the job, but was intrigued by his suggestion that we meet at the ticket counter in Churchgate. I had no idea what he looked like, or how he would spot me in the usual mob milling around. Through him I met Gieve Patel, Kamala Das, Dom Moraes and others. I feel privileged to know/to have known all of them.

I wish I could remember more about the days in the seventies when I began writing poetry. A.D. Gorwala of the little magazine *Opinion* published some of the early 'Catholic' poems, as did *Vrischik* which was published in Baroda, and the then new supplement of the *Times of India* accompanied by Mario Miranda's cartoons which, according to a poet friend, unfortunately took some of the bite out of the poems. In the mid-seventies Melanie Silgardo, who was at St. Xavier's, Mumbai, and I organized readings at which both established and newer poets read their work.

At a conference in Delhi, the Australian poet A.D. Hope asked me to send him whatever I had written (I hadn't published a book yet), and wrote me a morale-boosting letter about the poems. I needed that boost because at the same conference a Canadian academic told me that my poems weren't really poems because they didn't have images. This worried me because I was already unsure of the rather jagged pieces I had produced when all I wanted to write were lyrical poems with soft, sensuous and passionate lines! Regardless of what I told my students, only lyrical poetry seemed like 'real' poetry to me. Even when Adil Jussawalla said that the poems themselves were images, fixing people and situations at a 'decisive moment', it took me a long time to be convinced. It wasn't until the second book was published that I began to feel I was a poet.

So I was astonished by the response to the poems in *Fix*, particularly those which expressed ambivalence towards a parent. These responses sometimes came from people who did not always read poetry. This sense of being able to relate to people through my work meant a great deal to me as a person and as a poet.

The creative process being what it is, I don't really know where the poems came from. But I am endlessly grateful that they turned up.

Eunice de Souza, 2009

Eunice de Souza. Photograph by Madhu Kapparath

From *Fix* (1979)

Catholic Mother

Francis X. D'Souza
father of the year.
Here he is top left
the one smiling.
By the Grace of God he says
we've had seven children
(in seven years)
We're One Big Happy Family
God Always Provides
India will Suffer for
her Wicked Ways
(these Hindu buggers got no ethics)

Pillar of the Church
says the parish priest
Lovely Catholic Family
says Mother Superior

the pillar's wife
says nothing.

Marriages Are Made

My cousin Elena
is to be married.
The formalities
have been completed:
her family history examined
for TB and madness
her father declared solvent
her eyes examined for squints
her teeth for cavities
her stools for the possible
non-Brahmin worm.
She's not quite tall enough
and not quite full enough
(children will take care of that)
Her complexion it was decided
would compensate, being just about
the right shade
of rightness
to do justice to
Francisco X. Noronha Prabhu
good son of Mother Church.

Feeding the Poor at Christmas

Every Christmas we feed the poor.
We arrive an hour late: Poor dears,
like children waiting for a treat.
Bring your plates. Don't move.
Don't try turning up for more.
No. Even if you don't drink
you can't take your share
for your husband. Say thank you
and a rosary for us every evening.
No. Not a towel *and* a shirt,
even if they're old.
What's that you said?
You're a good man, Robert, yes,
beggars can't be, exactly.

Sweet Sixteen

Well, you can't say
they didn't try.
Mamas never mentioned menses.
A nun screamed: You vulgar girl
don't say brassières
say bracelets.
She pinned paper sleeves
onto our sleeveless dresses.
The preacher thundered:
Never go with a man alone
Never alone
and even if you're engaged
only passionless kisses.

At sixteen, Phoebe asked me:
Can it happen when you're in a dance hall
I mean, you know what,
getting *preggers* and all that, *when*
you're dancing?
I, sixteen, assured her
you could.

Miss Louise

She dreamt of descending
curving staircases
ivory fan aflutter
of children in sailor suits
and organza dresses
till the dream rotted her innards
but no one knew:
innards weren't permitted
in her time.

Shaking her greying ringlets:
'My girl, I can't even
go to Church you know
I unsettle the priests
so completely. Only yesterday
that handsome Fr Hans was saying,
"Miss Louise, I feel an arrow
through my heart."
But no one will believe me
if I tell them. It's always
been the same. They'll say,
"Yes Louisa, we know, professors
loved you in your youth,
judges in your prime."'

Mrs Hermione Gonsalvez

Mrs Hermione Gonsalvez says:
In the good old days
I had looks *and* colour
now I've got only colour
just look at my parents
how they married me to a dark man
on my own I wouldn't even have
looked at him. Once we were going
somewhere for a holiday and I went on
ahead my hubby was to come later
and there were lots of fair
Maharashtrian ladies there and they
all said Mrs Gonsalvez how fair and
beautiful you are your husband must be
so good-looking too but when Gonsalvez came
they all screamed
and ran inside their houses
thinking the devil had come.

Bandra Christian Party

Hubby emerges from coal bin
bottles under arm
face a smirk.
Hot stuff, he says.
The gathered goans giggle.
Dirty jokes:
hot stuff and sex.
Fred the comic slaps hubby
on back
now the party'll go men go
says Fred
goans agaggle
Fred laughing loudest
(he's the big thing
this side of Hill Rd)
What personality says Dominic
such pink lips men and
look at that chest
so comic says Mabel
keeps the crowd going
says Hetty
Fred is the life of the party.
Come on men Fred give us
a song calls Mabel
What personality says Dominic
such pink lips and look
at that chest.

St Anthony's Shrine

The beggars line up early
cry unrelentingly for alms.
The faithful come bringing
flowers, candles, money,
and pray for lost handbags,
lost souls, lost jobs.
Last week there was a miracle.

Alleluia D'Souza
Founder of the Shrine
emerges at ten.
'Alleluia, Mary Gomes'
mother is dying.
Alleluia, my son
found a house.
Alleluia, pray for me
to St Anthony.
Alleluia, my wife's returned.'
Alleluia stands by the shrine door
with bread she has
baked and broken.
'Take my child,'
She says to each,
'This is the bread
St Anthony has given.'

'May the bread turn to
scorpions,' says the parish
priest. 'The people miss Mass
but not St Anthony's.'
The bishop says, 'Alleluia
is a good soul. She donated
a Frigidaire last year to the
orphanage.'

Anniversary

Today, in his honour,
Mrs Lobo will not quarrel
with Mrs Lopez
about who should decorate
the altar and how.
The Men's Sodality will bring him
a box of cigars as they've done
for twenty years.
The girls of the parish will sing
May Your Path Be Strewn With Roses.

He sees it still:
I shall be a colt
mother when I grow up
a colt untamed
striking fire off rocks

his mother weeps
not knowing why.

Varca, 1942

The Archbishop said:
Great landlords and peasants
must worship together
The peasants cannot walk to a church
an hour away
So the great landlords of Varca
shot at their Archbishop

And the Archbishop
barred the Church doors and said
No landlord will enter the Church
in Varca or any other Church
in Christendom again
Devils will not be cast out
of the newborn
the dying will not be blessed
with holy oils

After many months
the Archbishop relented
and the landlords repented
and everyone worshipped together

And the landlords were landlords
and the peasants peasants
ever after.

Conversation Piece

My Portuguese-bred colleague
picked up a clay shivalingam
one day and said:
Is this an ashtray?
No, said the salesman,
This is our god.

Idyll

When Goa was Goa
my grandfather says
the bandits came
over the mountain
to our village
only to splash
in cool springs
and visit Our Lady's Chapel.
Old ladies were safe
among their bags
of rice and chillies,
unperturbed
when souls restless in purgatory
stoned roofs
to ask for prayers.
Even the snakes bit
only to break the monotony.

Omen

Today
that utterly respectable
big brown clock
in the college staff room
decided to move its hands
backwards.
No one is surprised.

My Students

My students think it funny
that Daruwallas and de Souzas
should write poetry.
Poetry is faery lands forlorn.
Women writers Miss Austen.
Only foreign men air their crotches.

Poem for a Poet

It pays to be a poet.
You don't have to pay prostitutes.

Marie has spiritual thingummies.
Write her a poem about the
Holy Ghost. Say:
'Marie, my frequent sexual encounters
represent more than an attempt
to find mere physical fulfilment.
They are a poet's struggle to
transcend the self
and enter into
communion
with the world.'

Marie's eyes will glow.
Pentecostal flames will descend.
The Holy Ghost will tremble inside her.
She will babble in strange tongues:

'O Universal Lover
in a state of perpetual erection!
Let me too enter into
communion with the world
through thee.'

Ritu loves music and
has made a hobby of psychology.
Undergraduate, and better still,
uninitiated.
Write her a poem about woman flesh.
Watch her become oh so womanly and grateful.
Giggle with her about
horrid mother keeping an eye
on the pair, the would-be babes
in the wood, and everything will be
so idyllic, so romantic
so *intime*

Except, that you, big deal,
are forty-six
and know what works
with whom.

He Speaks

Well, now tell me
what would you do to a
woman who wrote to you
saying: You haven't written
for three weeks. You're the
meanest man alive. Not even
an exclamation mark at the end
and she sends telegrams and
express letters saying it was
a joke, love, it was a joke.
I did what any self-respecting
man would. I ignored her for
a week. Her pleadings wore
me down. She was an affectionate
creature and tried hard, poor dear,
but never quite made the grade.
She *would* walk too close to me
and then protest naively: How
should lovers walk? Show me.
Ridiculous, too, her unseemly
mirth when I said confidentially
I have such an hypnotic effect
on women. Everywhere I go
they fall into my arms.
Jamie Bond! she cried
My man is India's answer to
Jamie Bond!

After that pathological display
I decided there was only one
thing to do: fix her.
The next time we were making love
I said quite casually:
I hope you realize I do this
with other women.

For a Child, Not Clever

Once you thought it good
you came fifty-sixth in class
out of fifty-six children.
But Mummy, you said,
fifty-six is bigger than one.
Voices crackle and break
around you. Why do you provoke
your sisters? Why do you never
tell us about your tests?
To me, the cousin who visits
sometimes, you say, as if
explaining things: I'm not clever,
you see, that's why these things
keep happening.

You have pierced me with your pain
dunce dunce double 'd'
Suddenly I see
how it's possible in Gethsamene
to say: I am the one you seek.
Let the rest go free.

My Grandfather's Death

They didn't nail down the lid
of the coffin, in front of us.
Nobody insisted I throw gravel.
They left him a little while
in the quiet February sun.
They were kind.
They didn't frighten anyone
make anyone feel how they'd
suffocate there
though they were dead.
Thirty years ago they
buried my father there.
That was a different kind of
death. They didn't know
I often asked
'What have they done to my daddy?'
and that nobody could explain.

Forgive Me, Mother

Forgive me, mother,
that I left you
a life-long widow
old, alone.

It was kill or die
and you got me anyway:
The blood congeals at lover's touch
The guts dissolve in shit.

I was never young.
Now I'm old, alone.

In dreams
I hack you.

For My Father, Dead Young

I hold the child up in delight.
The revolving fan cuts her through.
It's a dream.
I'm you.
I heard your fumblings in the dark.
Woke on wet beds.
Kniving marshes
I'm you.
You're the cold wind.
The grey mist.
The black dawn. The grinning skull.
I'm you.

de Souza Prabhu

No, I'm not going to
delve deep down and discover
I'm really de Souza Prabhu
even if Prabhu was no fool
and got the best of both worlds.
(Catholic Brahmin!
I can hear his fat chuckle still)

No matter that
my name is Greek
my surname Portuguese
my language alien.

There are ways
of belonging.

I belong with the lame ducks.

I heard it said
my parents wanted a boy.
I've done my best to qualify.
I hid the bloodstains
on my clothes
and let my breasts sag.
Words the weapon
to crucify.

This Swine of Gadarene*

This swine of Gadarene
has stopped his hurtle
to the sea.
No. The demons
haven't lost interest in him.
He feels
posthumous.
Behind him
the dead land.
Ahead
the dead sea.
For a little while yet, he says,
let me chew stubble.

*A district south-east of Galilee. Christ cured two men possessed by evil
spirits here and compelled the devils to enter a herd of swine which then
threw themselves off a cliff and were drowned.

Autobiographical

Right, now here it comes.
I killed my father when I was three.
I have muddled through several affairs
and always come out badly.
I've learned almost nothing from experience.
I head for the abyss with
monotonous regularity.

My enemies say I'm a critic because
really I'm writhing with envy
and anyway need to get married.

My friends say I'm not
entirely without talent.

Yes, I've tried suicide,
I tidied my clothes but
left no notes. I was surprised
to wake up in the morning.

One day my soul
stood outside me
watching me twitch
and grin and gibber
the skin tight
over my bones

I thought the whole world
was trying to rip me up
cut me down go through me
with a razor blade

then I discovered
a cliché: that's what I wanted
to do to the world.

One Man's Poetry

Irony as an attitude to life
is passé, you said.
So be it, friend.
Let me be passé and survive.
Leave me the cutting edge of words
to clear a world
for my ego.

The rage is almost done.
My soul's almost my own.

Chances are
my father himself
didn't wish to die.

My mother watched by his bedside
and never forgave herself
for being asleep
the night he died.
He left a desk, a chair,
a typewriter and a notebook.
At family gatherings
my mother smiled
in her best faded chiffon
and travelled third
with her in-laws travelling first
in the same train.

As I grew up
I longed only
to laugh easily.
All that emerged
was a nervous whinny.

My limbs began to scatter
my face dissolve
my love would hold me close
for hours when I could
neither speak nor weep,
bring me food and feed me.

From him I am learning to love.

Early Unpublished Poems

At Veena's Wedding

There are no happy rebels, you said.
Settle down. Don't cut your nose
to spite your face.

Watching you touch your father's feet
the glow of gold in your hair
I too feel joy
in the unbroken gesture

I too was dandled
on a father's knee
watched worlds
revolve around me.

Star-Gazing

The light I saw in you
love
came from a dead star.

I am to blame for this:
star-gazing at my age
is an ambiguous art.

I Want a Father

I want a father;
always have.
God won't do.
He's too judgemental.
And so I found you—

Like my father, absent.

Fledgling

I am grateful
the sparrows have made
my house their home.
All those months they stayed away
I waited for their return.
Soon the fledgling will cling
wide-eyed, to the pelmet
as generations of wide-eyed fledglings
have done.
The mother scolds and chatters
forgetting
shadows which circle the sun.

Rowanlake

Only the skin under your eyes
tells me you are older.
We could have been happy, you say
in India or Brazil. You still want
to wring your mother's neck.
You want to know if you
ruined my name.

It's your little daughter now
who tries hard to make me feel
ill at ease.
I can be polite to mother and daughter—
in twenty years one learns
all sorts of things.

Your pleasure in this meeting
comes when at long last
I am alone but unafraid.

Untitled

It's too late for me
to die young
as you did.
You left no words
to teach me
the secret of your courage.
I cling to little things—
a glossy new leaf
a singing bird at dawn
I close my eyes
on the long train rides
through this crumbling city
I convince myself
this method's painful
that one messy
that living does not desecrate
your memory.

Grandmother

My grandmother was fourteen
when she married.
We've lost that photograph of her
with gold combs in her hair.
She was beautiful
bore seven children
and often ran home
to her mother.
She and the servants
spoke the same language
of silence.

Family Gossip

St Christiana lived long before
ODORONO made the scene and
St Christiana hated
the smell of people.
It made her nostrils quiver
just to see them coming
and even their best friends
didn't tell them
to stop crowding her.
So what could she do poor thing
but take right off
and hover near the ceiling
in a rage.
But bless me if they didn't
just stand there
gawping.

Untitled 2

He's married, has a child,
another on the way—
is proud his family has been here
for generations
before the hills were quarried
and trees torn up by those
who could not count the years
it takes a tree to grow.
He finds my style a trifle hard, but
understated, urbane, witty.
I understand the call of child, and tree
and mountain spring:
He hasn't learned their language yet,
will freeze if I say
I need you, hold me.
His strength, cast-iron fidelity.

From *Women in Dutch Painting* (1988)

Women in Dutch Painting
(for Melanie Silgardo)

The afternoon sun is on their faces.
They are calm, not stupid,
pregnant, not bovine.
I know women like that
and not just in paintings—
an aunt who did not answer her husband back
not because she was plain
and Anna who writes poems
and hopes her avocado stones
will sprout in the kitchen.
Her voice is oatmeal and honey.

Pilgrim

The hills crawl with convoys.
Slow lights wind round
and down the dark ridges
to yet another
termite city.

The red god rock
watches all that passes.
He spoke once.
The blood-red boulders
are his witness.

God rock, I'm a pilgrim.
Tell me—
Where does the heart find rest?

Monsoon Journey

This time the mountains
were hidden by mist.

My lover is like smoke
my dearest friend far away

He writes with so much love
of the undiminished pleasure
of the text
the cadence and economy of poetry
of skies warm and generous
and of Simone Weil who says
grace fills empty spaces
where there is a void to receive it.
It is grace itself
which makes this void.

We are on the brink.

The Hills Heal
(for Veronik Jussawalla)

The hills heal as no hand does.
The heart is stilled by the blue flash
of a lone jay's wing.
Impossible to forget, you think,
the shadows of the sun here ever purple,
the receding plains where the wind still blows.

Yet the world will maul again, I know,
and I'll go gladly for the usual price,

Emerge to flay myself in poems,

The sluiced vein just a formal close.

She and I

Perhaps he never died.
We've mourned him separately,
in silence,
she and I.

Suddenly, at seventy-eight,
she tells me his jokes,
his stories, the names of
paintings he loved,
and of some forgotten place
where blue flowers fell.

I am afraid
for her, for myself,
but can say nothing.

I Choose Not to Marry You, Love

I choose not to marry you, love.
There is poison in my tongue.
I maul. I calcify. I am a rib again.
I touch the world.
Stars turn black holes.

Eunice

Eunice, Embroidery Sister said
this petticoat you've cut
these seams
are worthy of an elephant
my dear

Silly bra-less bitch

Eunice is writing bad words sister
she's sewing up her head
for the third time sister

the limbs keep flopping
the sawdust keeps popping
out of the gaps
sister.

Remember Medusa?

My dumb ox loyalty is
the frozen heart
the frozen stare
of long aloneness
unpeopled even by terror

Remember Medusa,
who could not love
even herself?

Better the flailing
the angry words
burning through the brain
the certain sorrow

than letting go than the fall
slow-motion
into that abyss

Each life-line of words
years in the making.

Another Way to Die

Being eaten by maggots
is fantasy

The real thing is
to touch the outlines
of the hands, the hair
to find no body there

In a few hours
or a few days
the bits reassemble
a breast flies back
a dull pain
where the heart should be
an ache for a touch
or a quarrel

For a while again
you are almost
human.

For S. Who Wonders If I Get Much Joy Out of Life

As a matter of fact I do.
I contemplate, with a certain
grim satisfaction
dynamic men who sell better butter.
Sometimes I down a Coke
implacably at the Taj.
This morning I terrorized
(successfully)
the bank manager.
I look striking in red and black
and a necklace of skulls.

Alibi

My love says
for god's sake
don't write poems
which heave and pant
and resound to the music
of our thighs
etc.
Just keep at what you are:
a sour old puss in verse
and leave the rest to me.

Advice to Women

Keep cats
if you want to learn to cope with
the otherness of lovers.
Otherness is not always neglect—
Cats return to their litter trays
when they need to.
Don't cuss out of the window
at their enemies.
That stare of perpetual surprise
in those great green eyes
will teach you
to die alone.

Reprieve

This poem is for you.
It's a reprieve.
It says
nothing in your little black heart
can frighten me,
I've looked too long
into my own.
Thank you for the gift
of your uncertainties.

The Road
(for Deepak Ananth)

As we came out of the church
into the sunlight
a row of small girls
in first communion dresses
I felt the occasion demanded
lofty thoughts.

I remember
only my grandmother
smiling at me.

They said
now she wears lipstick
now she is a Bombay girl
they said, your mother is lonely.
Nobody said, even the young must live.

In school
I clutched Sister Flora's skirt
and cried for my mother
who taught across the road.
Sister Flora is dead.
The school is still standing.
I am still learning
to cross the road.

From You I Have Understood

From you I have understood
something of the silence of gods
how they tire of being the first cause
of every quarrel
how they shrink
from sweaty importunity.
Even the skies these days
are full of junk in orbit.

Be less like the wild gods, love.

Unfinished Poem

I found your unfinished poem:
There's a sun in the sky
and you are near me
and all should be right with the world.
But something hasn't set
(and it had better not be the sun!)
I could pinch a line from Neruda for you:
'I want/to do with you what spring does/
with the cherry trees.'
There you have it: the apparent ease
of love and poetry.

October 30, 1987

For you I wrote
'I don't need words
any more.'

Now garrulous
with memories.

Songs of Survival

I
Don't write of self?
Self is a survivor-casualty
moan-mongering tragi-comedy
recalcitrant matter
mixed metaphor
struggling to breathe
in an odour of sanctity.
Trees are dusty
but condoms are blue.
Self detests platitudes.
Like you.

II
jackself
I can bludgeon you
no more

take pity
say forgive

Let me grow
as the grass grows

stanch
the primal wounding

jackself
say forgive

III
Nothing is ever still:
Rocks move. Rivers move.
Time passes.
Allow me my tailspin.
One day I'll find my axis
and revolve around the sun.

IV
Don't flail.
Don't let the hurt show.
Not even this afternoon
can last forever.

Perhaps you'll hear kindness
in a casual greeting.

Practice grave courtesy:
there are no tears in the
eye of the storm.

Survive to know you can.
There is little to be said
for suffering.

Songs of Innocence

I
Who made you?
God made me.
Why did he make you?
To know him, to love him
to be happy with him forever
in this world and the next.

II
orange berries in the backyard
goldfish in the pond
the sun high in the sky
uncles who make you feel tall

no myth in such memories
no chill in the dawn
marigold mood
before the fall

III
I crave your dream of innocence:
a profusion of flowers blooming
for themselves
birds big enough to swallow avocado stones

But green can be
humid as the womb . . .

Avoid, friend, the man who has never known
a dry season.

IV
Searching for roots
I find the caretaker dead
the white ants burrowing
grand-aunt clothed in cobwebs.

Her clock
crumbles in my hands.

Pink cement houses
surge up among the fronds.

I hear the pigs forage
and know this is not home.

This never was home:
grandfather left as a young man . . .

He had a well of sand.
To him more sand was given.

Transcend Self, You Say

Transcend self, you say.
Connect with myth, history,
the world crumbling around you.
Men can, and do. Beggars survive.
Destitutes survive. There's something in this culture.

Must ask beggars how they do it.

Smart arse. Poetess.

Friend, the histories I know aren't fit to print.
Remember Padma, widowed at seventeen,
Forbidden to see the sun for a year,
allowed out to crap only at night
when the pure were out of the way?

The perfect book is
one long cry in the dark.
A novelist said that,
who spent his life wondering why,
when the Nazis came,
his mother pushed *him* into a closet,
and let his sisters go to Auschwitz.

Meditation

The lonely ask too much and then
too little
chill the air with intensities
of longing or self-diminishment
cannot decide which is worse
the insularity of confidence
or the insularity of isolation
are hectored by those who've found
the motto in the cracker barrel
know kindness from those who
sometimes take risks.

Don't Look for My Life in These Poems

Poems can have order, sanity,
aesthetic distance from debris.
All I've learnt from pain
I always knew,
but could not do.

And She Lived Happily

And she lived happily ever after.
Or perhaps reasonably happy
for some of the time.
Infancy and grand passions
are exhausting modes of seeing.
Now the grey sky is a sky
not a pall
the crocuses are allowed
their hesitations
friends and lovers
their friends and sometimes
even their lovers.
As the days grow longer she sees
students, friends, mother, aunts,
not always there,
but on call, often enough.

Visit

I like to visit you, you say.
You're always calm and smiling.

Should I tell you, I wonder,
I was a burly little girl
who knocked her sissy cousins down?

Unsure of your welcome
you entertain me with stories
of kleptomaniac uncles
and bootlegging aunts
the laughter suddenly dying
in your throat.

Have I seen, you wonder,
a shot dog drag its entrails home?

For Rita's Daughter, Just Born

Luminous new leaf
May the sun rise gently
on your unfurling

in the courtyard always linger
the smell of earth after rain

the stone of these steps
stay cool and old

gods in the niches
old brass on the wall

never the shrill cry of kites.

Home for the Aged, Sydney

They came into the world stone cold,
faces furrowed with dark rain.
Nobody called them.
They have no history.
More chilling than fiction
the lives of those
so marked for sorrow.
The sun rises and sets,
rises and sets.

Five London Pieces

I
Wintering in London

I can't feel the edge of my sari
and stumble
a stump in shoes.
My coat-sleeve knocks down
a glass of lager in a pub.
I ask for sherry at a party
where only white wine is served.
I long for the downs
which stay green in winter.

II
Encounter at a London Party

For a minute we stand blankly together.
You wonder in what language to speak to me,
offer a pickled onion on a stick instead.
You are young and perhaps forgetful
that the Empire lives
only in the pure vowel sounds I offer you
above the din.

III
Meeting Poets

Meeting poets I am disconcerted sometimes
by the colour of their socks
the suspicion of a wig
the wasp in the voice
and an air, sometimes, of dankness.

Best to meet in poems:
cool speckled shells
in which one hears
a sad but distant sea.

IV
A Good Day

It's been a good day.
My lover has been
unusually witty.
I have found a new
Baudelaire.
The poet next door has told me
some disgraceful stories.
My muse is tapping out a message
on my Olivetti:

at least today
write a poem with some
fizz in it.

V
In Wittersham
(for Ruth Fainlight)

Peace is a wide, flat, silent marsh
with fat sheep grazing on it.
They're a special breed here
resistant to water underfoot
and anyway the marsh
has almost been drained.
I chat with a neighbour
about December roses.
A visitor here,
I want nothing to change.
Yet many planes are still found
in the marshes,
identification tags intact,
and the town five miles away
was sacked and burned three times.

Return

The old wrought-iron gate has gone
with the tall tangled grass
and the mosquitoes.
The priest is chanting his blessings
on the stone of the new building.
Squirrels chase each other up and down
the two mango trees left standing.

My neighbours want to know,
did I enjoy?
Thinking of the old wrought-iron gate
and the cotton tree
that managed only one flower every summer
I agree, perhaps enjoyment
should have no object.

II

It was the sound of the shehnai
in a London flat
that brought me scurrying back
to catch this train
to be again among
these old hills
stray bougainvillea
and the peasant women
with only a handful of berries to sell.

III

I covet the presence your home has.
I want to be like that:
cool, dark, subterranean.
There I would not covet even you,
grudge your many loves
or even write you more love poems.

IV

Sarla Devi, Kusum Bala, Rani Devi,
all of ill fame.
I read your story in
the morning paper:
you refuse to wear ankle-bells
worn for generations
you study law
you hear catcalls in the street
drums and bells behind your books.
Sitting alone in a Bombay restaurant,
listening to the innuendoes of college clerks
and a loose-lipped Spanish priest,
I know something
of how you feel.

V

Tuka, forgive my familiarity.
I have loved your pithy verses
ever since that French priest
everyone thought mad
recited them, and told us
of his journey with your people.
They have broken down whole streets
of houses in Pandarpur, to widen
the road to the shrine.
The priests do not sound like you
but I'll offer a coconut anyway
for someone I love.
You made life hard for your wife
and I'm not sure I approve of that.
Nor did you heed her last request:
Come back soon.

From *Ways of Belonging:*
Selected Poems (1990)

Notations

They needed so few notations
those unknown singers:
a dying queen, a faithless king,
a golden chain, the lover lost
in the dark forest of passion,
nobly lost, ignobly lost,
always they sang of loss.
No attempt to cauterize memory
no gestures of refusal
or acceptance. No cut to abstractions.
It happened: that is all they say.
It happened.

Aubade

So you are going too, my love,
the last, most beautiful
of my children:
a Botticelli, crystalline,
the pure ice-blue
of a southern ocean.

A line, a word, colour, rhythm
plangent in the mind's groove:
One sets them free—
to learn, finally learn
to claim nothing.

God Rock

There's a continent moving
under my feet, god rock.
In a million years
it will swallow the seas,
spew out mountains,
reduce this land
to a handful of gravel.

Give us a sign, god rock.

A city burns.

God Rock's Passion

God rock plunged into
the belly of the earth, molten.
Heaved off,
goat pellet seed.

Primeval slob.

Aravalli

The hills are splattered with
sacred linga, silicon-breast domes,
rivers sucked dry.
Predatory winds scorn paradox:
The hills are toads, fangs, skulls.
The chameleon, mottled grey like the rocks
barely breathes—
eyes half closed in meditation,
undivided in its aims.

Bequest

In every Catholic home there's a picture
of Christ holding his bleeding heart
in his hand.
I used to think, ugh.

The only person with whom
I have not exchanged confidences
is my hairdresser.

Some recommend stern standards,
others say float along.
He says, take it as it comes,
meaning, of course, as he hands it out.

I wish I could be a
Wise Woman
smiling endlessly, vacuously
like a plastic flower,
saying Child, learn from me.

It's time to perform an act of charity
to myself,
bequeath the heart, like a
spare kidney—
preferably to an enemy.

General Ward

'Imagine, she hasn't visited her mother
for three days!'
'What kind of daughter.'

Simple Christian sentiments,
simply kindly people who
plait the neglected mother's hair,
fetch her a glass of milk,
ring the bell for recalcitrant nurses.

How shall I say to them: in your simple words
I hear the subtle joy of
the guilt trip, the guilt whip?

Even the visitors in the ward,
confident in red and yellow taffeta dresses
feel their taffeta hearts go tsk tsk.

The Neglected Mother smiles at me
to pull me into the circle of sympathy.

Juhu Beach

So we visit my actor-friend in his home on the beach.
It's a squatter settlement, each home 5′ by 3′.
He can hardly stand up in it. We can't breathe.
I stub out my cigarette on a sandbag.

Ramu, a neighbour prepares the meal.
He used to be 'a joker' in the circus, but ran away,
couldn't take the threats, the beatings, the pay.

Through the gap that passes for a door
I watch the tide come in.

Once we had sat on a spot not far from here,
my actor-friend and I.
A stray dog adopted us and barked at passers-by.
It was my birthday. We feasted on pineapple cream pastries,
the dog, my friend and I.

From *Selected and New Poems* (1994)

Landscape

I

M. assures me she'll be back
to fling my ashes in the local creek
(We're short on sacred rivers here)

The pungent air will suit my soul.
It will find its place among
the plastic carrier bags and rags that float upstream
or is it downstream.
One can never tell.
The sea sends everything reeling back.
The trees go under.

II

We push so much under the carpet—
the carpet's now a landscape
A worm embedded in each tuft
There's a forest moving.

Everybody smiles
and smiles.

III

The crows will never learn
there is garbage enough for everyone:
the mouths of the young are raw red,
soundless.

The egret alights on the topmost branch.
Not a leaf is disturbed.
On all sides the ocean.

IV

Stretch marks of the city

Look the other way:
there are dhows there
Arab horses for desert kingdoms

An old monkey coughs in a tree

The young sense food
jump from rock to burning rock

We bar doors and windows
cower, nursing warm beer

An eagle hovers on a branch split
by lightning.

Otherness/Wise

I have spoken much of
otherness
and must now, alas,
practice what I teach.

Your poems are no longer
messages for me
and mine have become
an epitaph

for a late November afternoon
when the last rays touched
the leaves, the brass, the old teak chest,
and I forgot for a while
what an old painter friend taught me:

Forms without ache, he said, are futile.

So be it. Though I would have it
otherwise.

It's Time to Find a Place

It's time to find a place
to be silent with each other.
I have prattled endlessly
in staff-rooms, corridors, restaurants.
When you're not around
I carry on conversations in my head.
Even this poem
has forty-eight words too many.

Outside Jaisalmer

I

The sea receded. The dunes remember.
Trees have turned quietly to stone.

I watch two men bend intently
over a pawnbroker's scales

and think of you:

Walled city. Dead kings.
The tarred road melts where we stand.

II

Sixty miles from the border
stories:
the general on the other side
doesn't want war, he wants to
cultivate his poppy fields.

We're here to watch the sun set.
Birds fly in formation, and jets.

III

The life of the hero on the scabbard of a sword.
Faces in profile, erect penis in profile,
the colours raw, the rug in detail.
The milk he's washed in has turned a little sour.
Her hand touches her veil.
He looks into her eyes
she looks into his.
Behind the lattice work the waiting women
cry oh and stroke their breasts.

IV

We clatter over five river beds
broad, sweeping, dry
tour potters' weavers' villages
and Kuldera, deserted in protest
against a greedy king.
An old man brings out a few fossils
and says, Once there was a sea
(a hundred and eighty million years ago
but he doesn't know that).

The children say Hello
and look at my shoes.

From *Dangerlok* (2001)

Pahari Parrots

I

Not for him the cold swathes
of pine and mist,
hook-nosed king of a succulent sky.

In his wire-mesh cage
He gives nothing away.

I buy him on impulse.
He makes my flat his home:
Rubber plants, candles, pencils, plastic
make a fine confetti . . .

Princely wastrel of a
lost kingdom.

II

She peers through lattice windows
at the empty street
the long afternoon broken
only by the squawks of parrots.
The air is humid
but there is no rain.

III

Sometimes we compare notes:
I talk about the parrots
She talks about her children.
She tells me little K cries for effect.
If I get home after dark, I tell her,
They look at me with sad, reproachful eyes.

At dusk, all three of us and
all three of them
are melancholic.
Both want to sit on her lap.
Both want to sit on my left shoulder.
I smoke and down a vodka.

Soon I'll be a whiskery old lady
mumbling in my gums
hobbling about
two parrots in my hair.

IV

At the sight of Campari the parrots make
little weak-kneed noises.
Toth pulls the glass one way
Tothi the other
both hang on when I pull.
It's a regular bar-room brawl.

V

Spring, and the trees are translucent.
One can hardly tell
leaf from parrot
berries from beak
red splash on wing
from veins that tingle.

VI

Two trees and a garbage heap.
The garbage brings the barbets.
The parrots love the peepul tree.
There's a bulbul singing in the ashoka.
Throw in sparrows, crows and mynahs
you have your common city garden
complete with pandemonium at dawn.

The lady on the third floor says
We should cut down the trees
she can't sleep for the noise.

Lady, you're a fingernail
scratching a blackboard.

Later Poems

Mid-Sentence

You left mid-sentence—
Exam House, you said, that degree certificate . . .
I watched you turn the corner of the house, wave,
say you'd ring Sunday.
That was it.
Finis. Kaput. Dead.
Where you are there's neither harp nor halo
nor, what you preferred, an endless ashen dawn
beyond the reach of the sun.
It was thoughtless to vanish so suddenly.

My Mother Feared Death

I

My mother feared death,
hated black, and
doors, grilles, locks
that would not open.

Coffins, crematoriums.
No way to treat a lady.

II

Monsoon burials are a problem.
Coffins float up. Mourners slither
and slide on mounds of muck.

Habits die hard.
I'll phone her, give her the details, I think,
as I look at her with her eyes closed
and her mouth sealed with cotton.

III

My neighbour wants to know
what is to happen to my dead aunt's clothes,
so many of them new, her gold.

Who gets the pickings?
What colour was the coffin?

Death was not fastidious either.
It wrenched the intestines
riveted her eyes
locked her fingers over borrowed beads.

No, life's not cheap here.
Just unsubtle.

IV

Alive or dead, mothers are troubling.
Mine came back and said, 'I'm lonely.'
I left the windows open and the lights on.
She was buried in blue.
It remained. Nothing else did.
Handed back to us in a plastic bag
her bones are forced into a niche.
'I'm lonely,' she says.
I dream of her.
It's the best I can do.

Travelling

I

We walk to the shrine of the diamond-eyed god
This is the hour he's in green and gold
The women moan

He looks a little camp to me
upturned palm with rose
joss sticks burning

but oh those black granite thighs

II

Green roses on a terrace
lemon grass, a golden moon
a golden oriole chases a crow

Mine host waxeth sentimental.
Not a lover in sight.

III

The tattered balladeers invoke the
sun, the moon, the stars,
sing of kings who rode a night of sand
to plant a flag

on yet another sand dune,
of women who died when the sands shifted
in the wind.
A bulbul sings in the thorn tree.

IV

Wedged between houses, a sliver of sea,
casuarinas, clean sand,
infinity.

V

This town boasts a one-armed postal clerk
always drunk
a dog named Dumpy who can't stand the smell of drink
a street with three war widows and two light-eyed girls
who went astray
seven hen-pecked husbands
Copernicus who likes to treat his friends
and disappear when the bill appears . . .

Never underestimate a dishevelled town
the colonel says
reaching for the rum.

Sacred River

Two logs fastened in the river
for birds to take the waters
I saw no birds there
just a cremation or two on the ghats
onlookers at a safe distance
yet another pregnant half-starved stray dog
a white man playing at being a sadhu
top knot and all
But nothing stops faith
No. Nothing stops faith.
It will be heaven to get out of here.

Tothi

Tothi's back
Her beak slightly battered
Her panache intact.
She whistles for me from outside the grille.
I rush with offerings
of guava and melon.

Aunt

My aunt loves bright colours.
Widowhood be damned.
Ninety-one years be damned.
She reads the newspapers from
first page to last
looking for a cheerful story.

Reluctant Spring

The golden orioles have gone
The warblers are silent.
The last red leaf on the almond tree
refuses to fall.

Koel

Koel, stop those cries.
I can't take it this morning.
The wood-doves join your chorus of grief.

Look! The leaves are shining green
the sky a sort of blue
there's even a breeze from the sea.

We'll survive somehow,
Koel, stop those cries.

Invitation

She tempts me with a vision of hills
grass that's green
peacocks as common as sparrows

We can read in the courtyard, she says,
to the sound of the woodpecker working his tree,
admire her roses, pluck fruit, count stars.
Bring aunt, dogs, parakeet, she says,
write a happy poem or two.
Once in a way, she says,
we'll take a little walk to the village
to find out how the world's
not getting on.

Death

Under the dusty mango tree
ceremonial shaving of heads.
The newly bald make fun of each other.
The newly dead is an unknown quantity
urged on by the tuneless singing of the women,
and men in white standing their ground.

To a Naturalist

Mine's an humbler occupation,
hunting dog ticks, bed bugs, ants
whose steadfastness I can rarely match.
Fed up of concrete, a rat decided to
take up residence in my oven.
Watchman and broom soon settled him.
The wild parakeets chortle their way
through the seed box, three times a day.
As for the fat pigeons
pushing each other off my air conditioner,
there's no escape from their
orgasmic cries.